Muske, Carol,
1945-
Red trousseau.

$18.00

Red Trousseau

Red Trousseau

Carol Muske

VIKING

811.5
Muske

VIKING
Published by the Penguin Group
Penguin Books USA Inc., 375 Hudson Street,
New York, New York 10014, U.S.A.
Penguin Books Ltd, 27 Wrights Lane,
London W8 5TZ, England
Penguin Books Australia Ltd, Ringwood,
Victoria, Australia
Penguin Books Canada Ltd, 10 Alcorn Avenue,
Toronto, Ontario, Canada M4V 3B2
Penguin Books (N.Z.) Ltd, 182–190 Wairau Road,
Auckland 10, New Zealand

Penguin Books Ltd, Registered Offices:
Harmondsworth, Middlesex, England

First published in 1993 by Viking Penguin,
a division of Penguin Books USA Inc.

10 9 8 7 6 5 4 3 2 1

ISBN 0–670–84508–6
Library of Congress Catalog Card Number 92–50358
(CIP data available)

Printed in the United States of America
Set in Perpetua
Designed by Brian Mulligan

—for you, for the Muse

If I'm lonely
it's with the rowboat ice-fast on the shore
in the last red light of the year
that knows what it is, that knows it's neither
ice nor mud nor winter light
but wood, with a gift for burning
—Adrienne Rich, "Song"

Acknowledgments

These poems (or close versions) have been published in the following magazines or journals:

The Yale Review: "Field Trip"
The George Washington University Review: "In-Flight Flick"
Snail's Pace Review: "Theories of Education"
The American Poetry Review: "Red Trousseau," "Alchemy, She Said," "Stage & Screen, 1989," "To the Muse," "Insomnia," "My Sister Not Painting," and "Lucifer"
River Styx: "Unsent Letter Two"
American Voice: "Retro Vivo"
Field: "Prague: Two Journals," and "Last Take"
Poetry: "Kenya," and "Little L.A. Villanelle"
Colorado Review: "Barra de Navidad"

"Red Trousseau" was reprinted in *The Best American Poetry 1992,* ed. by David Lehman, Charles Scribner's Sons. (Guest editor Charles Simic.)

"To the Muse" was awarded a Pushcart Prize, 1992 (Pushcart Press, ed. by Bill Henderson).

"To the Muse" was reprinted in *After the Storm,* ed. by Jay Meek and F. D. Reeve, Maisonneuve Press, 1992.

I'd like to thank the following individuals for their generosity in reading and commenting on these poems in manuscript: Lynne McMahon, Michael Ryan, Jorie Graham, Bruce Lagnese, Erik Jackson, and David Dukes.

Contents

I

To the Muse

New Year's Eve, 1990

She danced topless, the light-eyed drunken girl
who got up on the bow of our pleasure boat
last summer in the pretty French Mediterranean.

Above us rose the great grey starboard flank
of an aircraft carrier. Sailors clustered
on the deck above, cheering, and the caps rained down,

a storm of insignia: S.S. *Eisenhower.*
I keep seeing the girl when I tell you
the *Eisenhower*'s now in the Gulf, as if

the two are linked: the bare-breasted dancer
and a war about to be fought. Caps fell
on the bow and she plucked one up, set it rakishly

on her red hair. In the introspective manner
of the very drunk, she tipped her face dreamily up,
wet her lips, an odalisque, her arms crossed akimbo

3

on the cap. Someone, a family member, threw a shirt
over her and she shrugged it off, laughing, palms
fluttering about her nipples. I tell you I barely knew

those people, but you, you liked the girl, you
liked the ship. You like to fuck, you told me.
The sex of politics is its intimate divisive plural,

we, us, ours. *Who's over there?* you ask—*not us.*
Your pal is there, a flier stationed on a carrier.
He drops the jet shrieking on the deck. Pitch dark:

he lowers the nose toward a floating strip of
lit ditto marks and descends. Like writing haiku—
the narrator is a landscape. A way of staying subjective

but humbling the perceiver: a pilot's view.
When you write to your friend I guess that
there are no margins, you want him to see

everything you see and so transparent is
your kind bravado: he sees that too. Maybe
he second-guesses your own desire to soar over

the sand ruins, sit yourself in the masked pit
and rise fifteen hundred screaming feet a minute
into an inaccessible shape: falcon, hawk—Issa's

blown petals? Reinvent war, then the woman's faithless
enslaved dance. Reinvent sailors bawling at the rail
and the hail of clichés: flash of legs on the slave deck.

Break the spell, reverse it: caps on the waves as they
toss away their uniforms, medals, stars. Then the girl
will wake up, face west, a lengthening powerful figurehead

swept gold with fire. The waves keep coming: the you, the me,
the wars. Here is the worst of it, stripped, humiliated—
or dancing on the high deck, bully-faced, insatiable.

Here is the lie that loves us as history personified,
here's the personification: muse, odalisque, soldier,
nightfall—swear to us, this time, you will make it right.

Stage & Screen, 1989

Disguised as a mutant,
my kid spins in the backyard.
She has the fly's compound eye
and that familiar flat robot
voice, hesitant, deflective: a human dial tone.
Her business is to rescue every person
recently changed into an insect.

Misunderstanding passion (the old poet told me),
a poem goes wrong in two ways: first,
like an amateur tragedian milking
the best lines of emphasis,
pushing quite innocent everyday dialogue

into enormity. Then what remains to be seen
can't be. Not the broken string of red glass beads
rolling under the table, the white chair pushed away,
the child's lidded, fearful sidewise glance—but look out
for the narrator's shadow falling on everything.
The images standing in for the self,

the fiery sky-divers stepping ahead of you into space,
first light on the row of talking monuments.
Outside, the mutant climbs the chinaberry tree.
Inside, a nostalgia for the not-too-human rears up,
groans, goes all trembly-fingered down the proscenium arch.

Outside again, she's just a kid in green mask and socks,
back on the ground, spinning. See what I mean?
The wind keeps blowing, it's hard-edged, shining,
self-contained as a struck pendulum. So pour
some coffee, go outside, feel something enormous, stop.

Field Trip

Downtown, on the precinct wall,
hangs the map of Gang Territories,
blocks belonging to the red Bloods
or blue Crips. Colored glass hatpins

prick out drive-by death sites—
as the twenty-five five-year-olds
pass by. They hold each other's hands
behind their tour guide, a distracted

man, a sergeant, speaking so far over
their heads, the words snap free
of syntactical gravity: *perpetrator,*
ballistic. The kids freeze in place,

made alert by pure lack of comprehension.
Then, like the dread Med fly, they specialize:
touching fingerprint pads and then their faces,
observing the coffee machine (the plastic cup

that falls and fills in place), the laser printer
burning in the outlines of the Most Wanted
beneath a poster of a skeleton shooting up.
It's not so much that they are literal minds

as minds literally figurative: they inquire
after the skeleton's health. To them a thing
well imagined is as real as what's out the window:
that famous city, city of fame, all trash and high

cheekbones, making itself up with the dreamy paints
of a First Stage Alert. The sergeant can't help
drawing a chalk tree on the blackboard. He wants
them to see that Justice is a metaphor, real as you

and me. Where each branch splits from the trunk,
he draws zeros and says they're fruit, fills each
with a word: arrest, identification, detention,
till sun blinds the slate. Not far away, through

double-thick glass, a young man slumps
on a steel bench mouthing things, a clerk
tallies up personal effects. Now he comes
to the gangs, how they own certain colors

of the prism, indigo, red—he doesn't tell
how they spray-paint neon FUCKs over
the commissioned murals. The kids listen
to the story of the unwitting woman

gunned down for wearing, into the war zone,
a sunset-colored dress. She was mistaken
for herself: someone in red.
She made herself famous, the way people

do here, but unconsciously—becoming
some terrible perfection of style,
bordering as it does, on threat.
The sergeant lifts his ceramic mug,

etched with twin, intertwining hearts,
smiling like a member of a tribe. Later,
on the schoolroom floor, the kids
stretch out, drawing houses with chimneys,

big-headed humans grinning and waving
in lurid, non-toxic crayon. Here is
a policeman, here a crook. Here's a picture
of where I live, my street, my red dress.

Our planet, moon. Our sun.

In-Flight Flick

The drunk next to her on the plane
holds up the photograph for her to witness:
an eight-year-old in braids
stolen away from him by an unspeakable
ex, through paid-for testimony.

Under her tongue, a milled tablet turns,
ready to separate the body from its terror
of motion, strapped to a seat
before a spread tray. His Scotch sits
jiggling in a cup-shaped niche, impaled

by a reading ray. His mouth opens
above the red slash of his silk tie.
He imitates, hand flat, a plane
taking off—*zoom*—so split

the wife and child. Then to show how
they broke him, he slumps in his seat.
Together, they watch his made-up plane
bank before the dropping movie screen.

Now it's dark. His drink flashes in the blue-
and-flesh beams shot from the credits.
His hands work in the air before Pompeii:
a long shot of ancient courtyards and whole

families frozen in domestic poses. One fall,
he says, flashing a wound, a torn screen scarred
him. He was only putting on storms.
Before us, the time-traveler turns an Uzi

on the plane, the robot girl cracks a smile.
Turbulence: the meal tray shakes under
the hand of the raconteur: one, two, three:
steak and rhubarb mousse. The air chops

like his hand, but all faces stay stubbornly
turned from him—including her face, daring him.
Every motion a betrayal, every gesture a fall into fire.

Theories of Education

These beads are hot, my daughter says,
lifting them gingerly from my neck—somehow
ignoring the obvious: they're pretty and they're red.

These are the days of pre-school entrance tests. Some
nitwit reads a *text,* asks kids to give it back verbatim.
The beads are hot, my daughter says,

touching the ring of red glass planets
warm from pooling at the throat's steady pulse.
Ignoring the obvious: that they're pretty, they're red—

she says instead what's usually left unsaid.
In her model galaxy, Earth pushes back Mars.
The beads (strung on hanger wire) are hot, she says:

aligned in sequence from the 100-watt bulb's too-
steady glare. *Hot* she says, moving Earth, moving Mars,
ignoring the obvious: one's pretty, one's red.

We can't say why our minds orbit this Earth, can we, kids?
Or why Mars looks mean as Hell! Blood leaps in the neck.
These beads are hot, my daughter says.
Ignoring the obvious: they're pretty. And they're red.

Frog Pond

Stuck pat with strawberry magnets
to her sub-zero are all the stages:
gill slits, lungs, sex—stopped
at the third month, when the fetus

is sucked out into a clear plastic bag.
Reaching in for a quick soda, you can almost
feel that flexible wind on your face.
The fetus (named *Jennifer,* it says)

develops in color-photo sequence till the second
trimester, when (more bold-face) the kid's
a murder victim, in cold blood, of Mom. You beckon
to nothing: milk cartons, cans, stand in the chill blast

of the suction door and grab your Sprite.
Day and night she stands outside the clinics
with the other Lifers. My advice: don't
take her on. I once learned phylogeny

provides intelligent options—but survival
does not necessarily select for insight.
Down the line: there's a smug printed
sign talking up adoption. Right.

So, knocked up, I'd owe my body to
an unforgiving god, who'd swallow my offspring
too? Here's a fat man rattling a bloodred
genie in a pickle jar. No wedding ring.

See that woman, head bent—they're hurrying her
through the police cordon, past the screaming faces?
I've walked where she's walking now—
and where she lies now, I once lay,

behind that secured door, near that white
waiting table. My mind divided, momentarily,
as if the world were just birth or no birth,
what I could or could not do and still seem

human to myself. Who first fixed in
my head that slashed membrane between life
and death? (I'd go toe-to-toe against her,
but she stops me cold with her small, past due

figure of remorse.) *God, what next?* she asks,
leaning against her icebox, her T-shirt
shouting how she pities the unborn. So do I.
But not as much as I pity her, quickening

with hate. And *love:* for those would-be
lives inbred to a set of family
gestures. One day on our way to the frog
pond, we take my daughter's hand saying

nothing—one on each side. She
asks me why I don't see what she believes.
I want to say *I do,* I see through all the cross-
wielding apologists to why she, alone in her kitchen, grieves.

It's sad. The big frogs croak like TV preachers
pad to pad. But look: at the pond rim
she points out tadpoles—hundreds, ink-black, legless.
See? we both say. My daughter kneels, tries to cup them

in her fist, but they're too fast. Born again and
again into the limits of our perception, they swim
intuitively, the way we think: she calls that
revelation. We're surrounded by the bull

chorus, a booming, backlit percussion. *Call
it revelation* she says aloud, and I won't, though
I'd call it the soul of a woman. Not the one she
discovers at conception. No, *this one,* this

power: split cell, sister,
this raw fixed light in her face set to mine.

Little L.A. Villanelle

I drove home that night in the rain.
The gutterless streets filled and overflowed.
After months of drought, the old refrain:

A cheap love song on the radio, off-key pain.
Through the maddening, humble gesture of the wipers,
I drove home that night in the rain.

Hollywood sign, billboard sex: a red stain
spreading over a woman's face, caught mid-scream.
After months of drought, the old refrain.

Marquees on Vine, lit up, name after name,
starring in what eager losses: he dreamed
I drove home that night in the rain.

Smoldering brush, high in the hills. Some inane
preliminary spark: then tiers of falling reflected light.
After months of drought, the old refrain.

I wanted another life, now it drives beside me
on the slick freeway, now it waves, faster, faster—
I drove home that night in the rain.
After months of drought, the old refrain.

II

Red Trousseau

"What is woman but a foe to friendship . . ."
—Malleus Maleficaram
(Witches' Hammer, *1494*)

I

Because she desired him,
and feared desire, the room
readied itself for judgment:
though they were nothing to
each other, maybe friends,
maybe a man and a woman
seated at a table
      beneath a skylight
through which light poured,
interrogatory.

II

Because his face always appears to her
half in shadow,
                    she chooses finally
to distrust him and her seared memory,

even though it was noon, when the sun
hovers in its guise of impatient tribunal,
seizing every contradiction in dismissive brilliance:

the white cloth, their separate folded hands,
a mock-crucible holding fire-veined blossoms. No,
it was a bowl of fruit, a glass of red wine,
the simplest, thoughtless vessel, that was it,
wasn't it, held up, like this, an offering?

III

Reading the accounts of the trials,
late at night, she sees that the questions
must have begun in a friendly, almost desultory
fashion: rising slowly in pitch and intensity,
to reveal, finally, God's bright murderous gaze,
the mouth of the trap. Conviction required stigmata,
the search for the marks of Hell's love on the un-male
body, the repetitive testimony of men: that she midwifed
the stillborn, curdled milk, spied, screamed at climax,
grew wings—and worse, *Looking over her shoulder,*
I saw her laughing he said *laughing at me*

till, at the end, days later, she could feel
her way eagerly, blind, cleansed of memory,
through the maze of metal doors to the last door:
                    the single depthless mirror.

IV

They were already disappearing, sitting there together
talking in a forthright way, laughing, unaware of their faces
reflected, enlarged like cult images, effigies:
dark hair, light hair. Already the ancient lens
sliding into place between them, whose purpose is not
to clarify sight, but rather to magnify, magnify till
                    its capacity for difference ignites.

        Tell me why it was only his gaze on her,
why his right to primary regard, *her* life under scrutiny,
her life reduced to some fatal lack of irony, naive midwife
                    to this monstrous *please?*

                See how the lens bends the light
into what amounts now to tinder . . .

                So sight can come, now, heatedly alive,
                        living wood, corrected

V

I admit now that I never felt sympathy for her,
as she stood there burning in the abstract.
Though condemned by her own body
(the ridiculous tonsured hair, bare feet
and bruised cheek, as if she'd been pushed up
against a headboard in passionate love)—
I suspected her mind of collaboration,
apperceptive ecstasy, the flames wrapped
about her like a red trousseau, yes,
the dream of immolation.

But look at the way her lips move—
it is the final enlightenment. Below
the nailed sign of her craft
                    are the words published
from her lover's mouth
the mouth of the friend who betrayed her:
her naked body, his head on her breast
like a child's, *heal me,*
and her answer?

God, tell me there was a moment
when she could have willed herself into language,
just once, into her own stammering, radical defense:

I am worth saving

before the flames breathed imperious at her feet
before her mouth, bewitched, would admit to anything.

28

Alchemy, She Said

Dross, she was like dross—
                    metal foam floating
on the ore melt. A wiseass hangover, like
                    Athena, that twisted nail
wrenched from the brow of male will.

                    She could imagine herself
as that same bitter excess of imagining, hyperbole,
                    afterthought's gall.

                    So what if, at those longago
dinner parties, the sconces dripped delicate moving wings,
                    if sometimes her words lit up
like cracks in the black lacquer of the mirrors. What beat

                    at her temples was experimental,
grotesque. Every idea of hers might be described as
                    shriveling flames dotting the radiants
of the mast, might be burning feathers and beaks caught in

the rigging, tossed up in that
blind flight battened to the first Saturday night she
was made up to be

something a boy had thought or wanted. That's when it
extended itself fully armed
from the brain. Coming down the carpeted steps
one at a time—

No woman would ever touch her, always overdrawn, drinking
with the bitchy boys
stirring their little city-states to war with the toe
of her sandal

as he had taught her.

But after the usual history, the blinding migraine of their
boring tête-à-tête,
Pallas, like a crone, bent over the heap of scorched alloys
stuck to the graven plate,

worrying the grist with her hands into attar, chrism
of such doubt, she herself could not believe. What
                        was left was a parthogyne,

time-traveler into and out of the cracked glass stadium.

Under the track lighting of the hated, blackened commandments,
her teeth chattering in her skull,
                        she stood in her high heels
in the snow as they shone headlights on her (that night,
                        that memory left), their
awful praise searing her neck many times like a white brand.

And much much later what was left on the workplate
was the first cell whose nucleus divided, divided brighter.

He was no longer there. She turned over in the bed,
pushed back the patterned sheets (a seaside hotel,
for once no elevators in the walls) and for the first
time let her own breathing interrogate the air.

If you listened, you could tell it was not the lie
of the ocean in the shell's convolvulus, what she
heard was not the sea, or the sound of the moving mast.
It was his cerebral muttering, the bit adjustment

inside her thinking which had suddenly, absolutely ceased.

My Sister Not Painting, 1990

I

My sister is painting not painting
slapping her brush across the air's smug expression,
          whipping pointillist grit
          ahead of her unseen broom

flung into the split hoof of the dustpan:
invisible pictures.
          Invisible man, invisible woman,
breath-colored bones, hair, cunt and cock.

          On the mirror she paints glass bricks,
each with a woman's face inside,
          mouth open, not screaming.

She flicks the brush, skin-painting
over her belly, over the unborn body within,
          future shapes of desire:
          arms, legs, sex, blinking heart.

She laughs: *Is this Minimalist enough?* I watch her,
drinking coffee. Somewhere, they're planning to pass
laws against mimicry—especially such extreme mimicry:
painting, not painting, birth, no birth at all.

II

This one is the most beautiful: a waterfall.
She painted herself here, standing just
behind the pour, a thin glassy sheet.
She was playing captive, winking:
red mouth, naked, necklace of dragonflies.

I remember that day and
this embarrassed meal,
the elongated utensils,
punctured orange sun.
She painted everyone's
anguished silence—
just after Uncle, drunk,
had disgraced himself
by telling his awful story.

She painted a parrot,
neon-green, on Uncle's head.
Shamed by his small vocabulary,
he couldn't help himself.
Two of his phrases were
Prove it and *Fuck Freud*.

The parrot, not the uncle.

III

He'd trained it. Was the parrot obscene?
He said other things: shit, hell, damn.
A family scandal. When he sat on Uncle's shoulder,
he projected his metal voice into Uncle's
human one, telling his famous story, helplessly,
after a shot or two. All of us staring into our plates.

Aunt Grace, his wife, drank gin fizz
from a tall glass, peering at
the clear, bloodcolored swizzle
stick like a thermometer.

      But there was no stopping him.
He was back in the World War, last one left
in his regiment, wintry Alps, everyone dead around him.
He buried no one, but waited days and days to be saved.
He dreamed they were alive in a different way. He sang.
Suddenly he saw a young man in a military uniform, standing
before him in a bright light. Then the youth's clothes
melted away and the boy became a woman.
         Uncle desired him,
desired to lie down with her among the dead bodies

of all his friends who had died for our country.
Then the man-woman turned away, then faced him again,
revealing the Sacred Heart burning in its cage
                              of neon thorns.

Carried at last down the mountain
to the hospital, he could not stop
seeing this, telling this.

                    So Christ was a woman
and he longed to fuck her. God is the two
sexes joined, he cried, spilling,
don't you see, one sex! joined at the heart!

IV

Till they held two wires to his temples
(obscenity, sacrilege) and he grew quiet,
walled up in the family business, a man
in a glass elevator—moving his jaws
enough to be male: some hellos, dirty jokes.
                    But a flurry of gestures:
hands pressed to his temples, dead thumbs on a buzzer,
fist raised, snatching at air as if he could
catch his story, lightning in the shifting,
cloudy synapses. He put out his hand for
a firm handshake, a backslap, then secretly raised
his middle finger, scratching his nose.

Years later, he looked up, seeing his niece
beside him, calmly sketching.
Not talking to him, just sketching,
the pencil tracing the shapes of the thorns
eating each other around that red and blue
                    beating suspension.

V

She lives in a little town. She's afraid.
She imagines herself facing some ignorant, powerful
tribunal:
                giving advice on how not to paint.
Terrific, she says, how *not* to paint this story:
Not paint *here:* the snow riddled with holes,
shrapnel pocks, little yellow lacework of piss
or *here,* not paint Uncle bearded, raving,
on his knees? Not paint *here,* his friend, the corpse,

boots and helmet, mouth open in song—half of
a silent aria, the cement duet of *pain, sky, pain,
sky*? Here. Not paint the soldier-Christ-woman
with her removable heart atorch, her black brassiere,
sheer black stockings?
                Not paint *here,* the center,
bruisecolored, tumescent, his bloody hand on himself?

VI

Well then, *not* the sky's flaming torso, sunset,
or the shaking puzzles of fire I saw when you slammed
the screen door's gold mesh between us—

                              years ago—
                              that summer dusk?

Not the blessed anarchy of your teasing face,
screaming *I can paint things you've never dreamed of!* Or
me, screaming back, yanking the door, wild
with joy and insult, *You mean the blind can paint?*

Then who will paint us noticing how
he stood there, across the lawn,
a glass burning in one hand? In the other,
the creature in its gold cage, all swirling feathers . . .

and the beak, the terrible slit tongue, don't you
remember? backing us up to what we'd always be?
Prove it—then the other thing, remember it? Or not?

                              the joke, the obscenity?

Kenya

I

Our spines went numb, stunned by the ruts,
rocking in the shockless poptop van
toward the animals, who stared back bored
into telephoto reduction. A bold-face notice flapping

on wire: No one allowed in the game parks
after dark. We'd seen what poachers left behind:
crumpled faces chain-sawed from the skulls
of live elephants, suckholes of hacked-out tusks.

We stood in the lodge, beneath the mounted heads
wearing leather boots, camera packs. Masks
lowered over doorways, fires. Open lion mouths,
their silent roar orbiting the room, till we

were deafened to every other sound, even
the discreet chime announcing our meals.

II

A little girl squats to pee; the Ground-
walking Hornbill stares at me with human
eyes under the gothic arch of trees. Maybe
the soul is that fiery shrug, shock,

lifting the heart up in its saddle:
the baby squats, her eyes blink, sick.
Long ago the priest told me we're an animal
bent to an enlightened will, but in fact we're

just a face, a brain behind it. The people trust no one,
they too have been hunted. They push their huts
up against the reserves, waiting days on end
for the migrations. So that they can follow,

followed by the picture-takers. The patterns
of Masai beads, red & white, fly up like blood-manes:
again and again the animal god being sucked at the neck.
In the ruins of the burned hotel stands the young man

with his magnet pot, calmly splitting hemispheres,
proving water runs in opposite directions a step
either side of the Equator. Something almost
apprehended is the soul, but the mind, stubborn, at war with

itself, tires. No shimmer of connection links these things:
how I come awake, terrified, to heart-shaped knots
in the mosquito netting. Light on the thatched ceiling,
a cup of black tea. This morning's headlined executions.

Black ink: my journal keeps track of what's odd—
                          white zebra, white rhino.

III

Faces floated in air: we photographed.
Piles of recovered ivory burned,
we could smell it on the breeze. The killers
kept coming. The souls of the elephants seemed

to be carving themselves out of air near a river
where they used to bathe their young. Still, no one warned
the people, who had painted white wings on their faces,
that we would photograph them. Three turned their backs,

crossing the river as it began to grow dark,
shapeless bundles on their heads. The owl spoke:
then the hawks, their runged sound hovering.
Then, singly, the ones crossing the river called out

shrill, stretching their long necks,
swimming now, the bundles on their skulls engraved
by moving shadows, dropped like expressions
from the shocked, intelligent face of the moon.

Insomnia

This room's walls are breathing fluttering gauze.
Beyond the black cautery, near the transparent
shelves where they store the remains: canned applause

from the TV—lit by waves of phosphorescence.
Loving the buzz of night's amputated touch, God swings
his red baton and no music soars. Already sunrise? Sense

by sense, we're dead. Stay up with me, no one ever does.
Nothing on the tube but battle hearsay, the flag's signoff.
Expressions I could use burn up like old photographs of faces—

a very cute Bible story full of sex and death.
God swings the guttering torch. Dawn, a razor
in its teeth, flashing adlibs, graffiti from Lethe.

These are not dreams. If I want dreams,
I'll press the keys. The night just isn't night
lit up like this, like day. Infra-red talking screens

just down the hall, let them walk a mile in my shoes.
I see us getting in the car, then ignition: the
flaming key held in the blackened, clenched fist. Bruise-

colored clouds. What comes on but backlit scrims
from history: the disintegrating image of the deranged
President's face, the green electrical storms

and the dangling key, the tribesmen running, on fire—
the scaffold, the chair, the stake, the ball turret, the pyre,
and my favorite, the wheel—remember the sweet, mindless

wheel,

expecting to be invented every night, again
and again, expecting to roll uphill
and down, cradle and bough,

expecting to be honored for its social nature, its dreams,
the salt hiss of the sleepless woman, in flames,

tied to its turning spokes?

Lucifer

Two A.M. and we're on Lucifer, arguing, drinking,
one of us a Believer. I say if that beautiful
light-named angel, once most loved of God,
fell, he must have kept falling into insight—
scattering his illumination, plummeting, coming apart
into a broken new deity, one that divides
as the woman's face in darkness,
the man's face in quick rip-slashes of light.
Starry dark: down and down She falls into her empty glass,
the night sky lights up with all He refuses to let go.

Prague: Two Journals

—Jan Palach, a Czech student, burned himself to death protesting the 1968 Soviet invasion of Prague

"AVENUE OF STATUES," CHARLES BRIDGE, 1970

Look at her, St.-somebody-or-other:
clutching her stone roses
like some ancient maid-of-honor.
A big girl who elbowed boldly up
to catch the bride's bouquet. She
caught the future: it wasn't hers.
        The statues tremble:

see it? a blue spasm, like a wave, breaking over
the rigid faces, the stone musculature. Eye-flicker
of intent, maybe the sculptor's last gesture
completing itself in the unsettled stone? What
        was just beyond the chisel's inference—

a long luxurious stretch, arms up, a yawn,
a bared breast. The shoe falls: what happened next.

History, like a bus, stopped and let us off
in a pool of some light substance, stones of air.

A little crowd of long-hairs,
after curfew, out of our depth—it slowly dawns on us,
we're somewhere important!

A trail of rose-lit tents on the horizon,
and these saints with their raised spears:
sunrise.

WENCESLAS SQUARE, 1990

Havel's face everywhere, my daughter's hand in mine.
The street jammed all the way to the National.
I look for a plaque, a sign commemorating
his death. An old man, a bureaucrat, quietly pops corks,
carves ice wedges into swans, dolphins, girls—
hunched over an old file cabinet he's wrestled
to the curb. Snowy commas curl from his knife.
No plaque. No sad past tonight. A street singer
tries sleight-of-hand, but her cards are frayed.
Heretics ignite the images. Years make clear
their courage: they stood alone saying there's
a better god or forget god—refine an image,
worship it, refuse to go blind: see my numbered face?
All this faceted chance: diamonds, hearts.
My daughter watches the parade of cards, marked. I remember
how they covered the spot where he burned with rough pine.
It became, nevertheless, an off-limits shrine.
What's in the file under his name?
            A pile of ashes. A glass of cheap champagne.

CHARLES BRIDGE, 1970

Hey Jude some kids intone at the sound of boots.
Did we think we'd go limp, recite Marcuse? Embossed flash
of a Red star, then a bullhorn's raised note.
We left right away. A student visa gets me to Kafka's grave,
but we're forbidden to sit among these thirty hooded figures,
or catch Z's like that sleeper in the shadow of a raised
stone axe, pass around hash in a flat pipe.
The weary mind closes its eyes behind the stone masks.

          I woke up, dreaming an eye painted
over the missing breast of St. Ludmila,
protector of the outsider, the circling soul.
I dreamed I saw Jan Palach's ghost.
Who'd nothing to say to us, though I watched him
for a sign as he crossed. Beneath his feet,

the bridge hovered like a spacecraft on its sixteen pillars,
built to last: pink-lit, spanning the Vltava.

FAUST HOUSE, 1970

In this house lived Edward Kelley, the English alchemist,
who transmuted gold at the court of Rudolf Two.
To a pound of boiling mercury, he'd add a single
drop of blood-red oil and beckon the court,
                    come see the brilliant grit in the pot!

Today soldiers reinforced the planks
over the spot. There was a girl there
who'd been his intimate. She cried but said nothing.
I saw his photograph, laughing. First the blood-red powder
added to the boiling contents of the crucible—
then you can just make it out
        through the colored smoke, bits of stars,
        spittle, a horse's bit, a blow to the sweet footman's skull:
                                        gold.

GOLDEN LANE, 1990

Alchemists' Lane. Mouse-houses, sixteenth century, frowning
under the castle arches. Goldbeaters, so called, fled here from
a fire. Up this diminishing street comes me, twenty years ago,
clutching my Duino Elegies. Flutter of silk at my neck. I could
recite all the once-resident writers: Seifert, Maranek, Kafka—
neighbors of Madame de Thèbes the fortune teller and a man who
                                    owned a circus of white mice.
Later, at the hotel, I call an old phone number and then another.
I put weight on one boot-heel, showing off my Bohemian ancestry,
college politics. Who would I be next? A voice says hello in Czech,
then speaks English. Palach put in his pocket: a political tract,
a poor flower. Then the flames re-made him. Hello. My name is
                                    Carol.

THE CLEMENTINUM, 1970

At the Clementinum, I am shown the Latin hymnal on parchment—
dirty words in Czech scribbled in the margins
by the noble ladies of St. George Convent. I'd give
my left tit to read this: Prague's earliest record of smut
written in the vernacular. By ladies. In a holy book. Well,
they were sick of the Empire, sick of the foreign liturgy.
Sick of being skirts. A pox on the rump of the fat Roman
priest! Jan Hus, the clear-eyed heretic,
threw out the sacristy's Papist gold.
Ladies, I give you the Roman Church, he said in Czech,
                                        and struck the match.

He burned fast, she said to me today, the girl who was Jan Palach's
                                                    lover.

THE INTERCONTINENTAL HOTEL COFFEE SHOP, 1990

In the Intercontinental Coffee Shop my daughter
rips her red lollipop free of a linen napkin,
reminding me suddenly of a rude passage I once glued
in an etiquette book. Something about the private parts
of Emily Post, a little kid's revenge—
though I still hate etiquette lessons. A jacket-back goes by,

the Soviet symbol with a bar through it.
Get it? says Annie, popping
her gum. *Down with red stars.*

Across the table from us is Jan Palach's lover.
In hat and scarf, though it's warm—
her face still young, but worn, like a book paged through
by cynics. She talks fast, catching up to an old self.

CHURCH OF OUR LADY OF TYN, 1970

Here's the marker for Tycho Brahe,
the Danish astronomer who believed the earth
was the center of the universe. *Better to be*
than to seem to be was the motto carved on his headboard.
Outside, a light rain begins to fall. The girl at my side
tells me that her lover stuttered, *a slight impediment*
she says. But when he sang foreign rock: Blowin'
in the Wind, Satisfaction, there was no hesitation.
That day he died, he sang a song
he'd made up. It rhymed but when she tries
to think of it, it's gone, even in Czech
there are only commas. Tycho set the self
a task: an orbit defied. So in the mirror, he saw the face
floating to the left in its ring of flames, detached.

I kissed his arms, she says, the little hairs stood up.
Then we went out together, into the street.

HOTEL INTERCONTINENTAL COFFEE SHOP, 1990

As she talks, I see her crossing the chalk lines
drawn shakily on the stones of the Square. He lengthens
beside her: the shadow of a flame on a wall. I see
the tanks, poking out their comic profiles. But then it's dim.
There was the place he walked to *in no uniform but the mind's fire.*
Then he turned from her, waving her back, waving away
the cheated, shouting executioners.

He kept touching himself, she said.
Over and over as if he was a newborn, finding
his body for the first time. Then he began to bow,
                       growing transparent.

                       My daughter lifts
toothpicks gingerly, one by one, from their chance
prop-up in the hotel ashtray, trying not to disturb
the stack's internal balance. Bored, she looks
where she sees us looking: sun touching the fragile

interdependent pile. *In no uniform but the mind's fire.*
What we are looking at took twenty years to imagine.
Then the pile collapses, as if sucked inward. It grows
dark outside as she begins to weep, the toothpicks
are realigned, gum snaps, *no red stars,* and he burns

before us, he goes on burning.

M. Butterfly

1

Onstage, the hero is arguing with his lover
of many years, a beautiful woman who has just
revealed to him that she is a man. Look closer!
She was born a man, but became perfect:

dependent on the soul's double-take. Unwound
like a chignon, shaken out like a plucked harp's
fan of gold: she's laughing, kneeling to pour tea.
She is too perfect, isn't she? each length of lacquered
nail clicking against mirrory surfaces that repeat
her made-up face wherever he looks for his own

set expression. She recoils,
then releases herself abruptly into his senses
like a fragrant gasp of the atomizer. He can't even
see she is a spy. Intercepting state secrets
he willingly reveals
late, over champagne, in bed, in the grip
of this committed self-caricature: love.
He's a career diplomat, she is

above nothing.

The plot: implausible but never exactly comic.
And a hero who is a fool, but such a scholar
of humiliation he begins to appear full of power,
                              an object of awe.

Now he paints a Kabuki mask over his face,
lifts a dagger, as his Butterfly watches.
When he cuts his throat, the audience catches
                                        its breath.

In his dressing-room, I wait out the curtain calls
leafing through a magazine: a wedding
in China where brides wear red. Her baby
face peeks, coquettish as sunrise, between
              the parted lips of a plum scroll.

        When he bursts in,
a face sweating from his face, the audience's
cries still audible in the walls, he turns to me
so that I can see that he is empty: there is nothing left

now that anyone, even a wife, could name.

2

And earlier in Act Two, the huge furled
scroll of Mao's face drops, forming the back-
ground as the Red Guard flings itself through the Middle

Kingdom and cruel children (the small actors) rule—
as they rule sex, our sexes.

God, let the poet forget
the pieces of the monolithic image! *Only a man* says Butter-
fly, can create the perfect woman.

Let the Peking Opera set fire to a single scene: dynastic
struggle, syncopated in places, but plainly erotic.
Isn't this what the acrobats flip backwards for, spin toward

like tops in their gold god-costumes:
the set-to at face level,
flaming whirling sticks?

And Butterfly looks like a pimp, after a clever gender
transfer into the courtroom scene. Weary little wiseass
in slicked hair, trendy suspenders—chatting
about East/West, race/sex, illusion and monkey-god real.

3

           Now the hero wipes off his make-up
at the lighted mirror and he is you—the footlight mike,
still on, eavesdrops over the speakers: murmurs of the exiting.

Now the fat bossy dresser disappears (with an ironic bow to me)
to launder your kimono. You and I look at each other in the mirror,
                        one gaze exiting into the other.

           Then people arrive. Champagne spills.
Later everyone troops, laughing, out the side exit
                   opening out onto Broadway

           —which can only be reached by crossing
the empty dark stage still littered with fake white flowers.

           I hang there looking out: silent perfect rows,

pick up one of the blossoms Butterfly flung about so
carelessly in Act One. Sobbing, dropping them at his feet.

                    Wanting him to see how, abandoned by him,
she is nothing—(the original opera readying her death!)
He turns away from her falling blossoms, but there's the eerie hope
she allows herself—born purely of acting—look closer,

born of her capacity to be . . . her own audience, and
his?—separate melodramas, his inviolate. It's true, he once
loved her and look at the earth's gifts of empathy: Rain falls, sun
rises. There is ritual. Look closer. If one learns mercy, even as
theater,
            one comes to expect it.

Character

We stand together on the dark stage
where earlier this evening
you raged, then fell down and wept

                    before a dream tribunal.
You wore camouflage, then cloth of gold.

Look at you, still standing
               staring out
               into the empty house

hypnotized by the light
as it shrinks up the center aisle
igniting the frayed torches of the narrow
                          carpet:

a single path of opening and closing nights.

How you strode to the footlights
at one point and talked so softly
and tenderly to us! I think what we felt
was simple gratitude for you, someone

behaving exactly as we expected, piloting us safely
through the snowy night. But character,
your character, had more to say, more to become—

and was bad finally, unforgivable. How could
you act this way? Our hurt perceptions swirled
about the proscenium and still you stood,

in the Third Act,

letting the lightning strike you—

turning those invented sentiments
as they began to burn, singly, in reverse—

back into flesh, hair: back into the audience's audience,
that betrayal of all human trust.

III

Unsent Letter

There was the dream: we each dreamed it.
It traveled into us,
                          like the intention
of an animal stalking us, or a god.
It came over us, a red shadow.

It did not move outward, like recognition,
          though it was a dream of touch
and touch demands double scrutiny.

There were no dream symbols,
not even the literal symbols of our lives:
what we worried about separately that day,
a child's lost toy, a ledger, two cracked
white tiles, each imprinted with a blue fleur-
de-lis, a dark silk necktie, unknotted, pulled free.

You were afraid of how the body
scorned the figurative.
          How right that you feared
what resisted transformation: what I recover of it now

is relentless—bed, dark covers, lamplight,
flesh against flesh. And nothing can stop
the non-echo,

         the absence of repercussive sound
that makes the present deafening.

It will always be the present in that place.

If you could admit only this: there was no way
to wake from that dream. The rest of it, you see,
is my work: slowing the mind's quick progress

from the hypnotic of that startled world
to the empty solicitation of metaphor,
the loathsome poetic moment.

Crows, naturally, look at them gathering!
Consecutive murderous insights,
like our life stories, assembled from
little convenient logics, strategies,

        slow death by interpretation.

Unsent Letter 2

You say you don't know who you are. I take
the plate of the homeless man and fill it
with macaroni and salad. Does he know who he is?
The next man comes up and I say "Would you like
a roll?" and he says "In the sand?" and laughs.

The next one is a woman, pregnant,
young. She asks in a small voice
if she can have some extra food.
We give her noodles, meat, greens.
She looks at her plate and begins

to cry. *I'm so tired,* she says
and stares into space, then at me.
I want to take her in my arms, but
I keep serving food, my hands in
the clear plastic gloves ice-cold

from the ocean wind. After a while
the pregnant girl has finished eating
with the others on the grass and wandered
away. I don't know who you are either.
We turned to each other,

                    once in blinding sunlight,
once in darkness. Going nowhere, in dream-quick
transit—as if we'd been abandoned
by our lives, cut free of every expectation of identity.

St. Augustine said to the crowd around the magus
that we do not understand miracles because we
do not understand the nature of time.

The magus collapsed duration: in his palm
the bean-pod unfurled into a shoot, flowered. I felt
your touch, not in time: in charmed space
where that seed accelerates, cycle by cycle.

And if we sped up transition—she'd have
another human being in her arms, an infant
—just like that—but she is homeless,
nothing to hold her outside her self.

He has left her, as we are all left, so we do not want
to hurry it, the miracle. It's better that it be served
in gradual sequence, do you see? —child, seducer, mother,
father, child, seducer . . . do you see? Faces: a food-line, a *you,*

one frozen location of mercy: a final divided portion
                                        to set on each plate.

Unsent Letter 3

(RETRO VIVO)

"I'm hot," says the biochemist. Shows me
the sectioned crystal ring and the tag around her neck
with the bit of film that slowly gets developed,
indicating she's cooked enough for time out.

                It's low dosage she says.
I doubt it. She wants to find a cure for cancer,
she wants to find out why cells replicate wrong,

she doesn't sweat the radioactive isotopes.
She reaches bare-handed under an oven hood
stamped with the yellow & black nuclear
triangles, ignoring the lead-lined gloves

on a hook above. I think of the picture of her kids
thumb-tacked up in her office, the crayon drawing
of mutant turtles by her youngest. I ask about slice enzymes,

it's for my book. Like molecular scissors she says
snip-snips her fingers in the air. The centrifuges hum.
Do you ever think about fate? I mean the way she does,
as if it was a chemical, recodable spiral inside us?

Figure your own mortality would matter less,
if you were outlived by one smart and lucky guess,
your name rippling in the gene pool? So what if you
light up like a Zippo, desire what ends by burning

you up: one narcotic spark, the fatal dream,
yes: what she feels, I've felt running through
my veins. I watch her, hand on her hip, half-grin:

terminally differentiated—that far down
the trail of the cure that will kill her.

Unsent Letter 4

LAST TAKE

I watch them killing my husband.
        Trained assassins, pumping round after
round from behind a camouflage truck:
        they crouch toward his crumpling form.

Under the white floodlights,
        blood jets sputter from his chest,
his head's thrown back. He shouts out a name, sliding down
        the white wall against the damp flag of his shadow.

A little guillotine shuts. Hands sponge the wall.
        He stands, alive again, so there's no
reason to fear this rehearsed fall, his captured cry,
        the badly cast revolution that asked his life.

The damask roses painted on the folding parlor screens
        of the phony embassy are real in a way, but the walls
are fake, and fake, too, the passion of these two naked human bodies
        embracing on the Aubusson: nevertheless, they obsess

the eye like any caress. Off-camera, the actor stroking his stubble
of beard, the actress's hands on her own small breasts.
Presented with the mirror of our sentiments, it seems
possible to believe that we love the world, ourselves—

Waiting in the wings like extras, full of desire
projected away from us. These sky-high fingers
of light imply, off hand, all night we stand in for God here.
There is nothing to fear, he gets up and falls down again

in slow motion. A boom swings into the frame,
then out. Loaded dice are shaken onto green felt before
the trembling hands of the unwitting victims. A roulette
wheel turns: the red, the black, chemin de fer.

The train crosses the border: inside, rows of people jammed
together, watch, weep. Like Art featuring Life, the real
sky behind the starry backdrop fills with stars. The lovers kiss.
I want to cry out How much? How much do you love each

other? But the director in his cherry-picker signals another take:
The sky grows light. It's late.

Barra de Navidad: Envoi

—*for my sister*

Up the narrow road
from Barra de Navidad
they came, rippling
        in the heat:

       women dressed as brides
children bearing blossoms,
their white skirts and veils
       blinding in the noon sun.

The cars stopped, one by one. Cold
inside our tinted glass interior:
       I rolled my window down.

       Insubstantial as a mirage,
they hovered, pure white, improbable as the place:
a bleached spit of earth slid between the old half-
       alive volcano perched above us,
              and the bay.

They had nothing to say.
Unwinding pale crowns of hibiscus
from their hair, they shook free the heavy petals,
       then parted to reveal

the young man with an infant's white coffin
on his head. He strode forward
                              intent,

the way a girl carries a water jug, one arm up,
in a perfect compromise of balance.
                              Undistracted

by our stares, he set his feet down against the white
bearers, the earth's sheer pall and compass—
                    his gaze set far beyond us.

Still, I saw how if a single red blossom had fallen in his path,
he'd have stumbled—
                    into the shadow of the raptor circling above
or into his wife's sudden keening
spreading like blood unpent beneath the heat's surface.

So little remains in this feeble re-telling:
        his regal stride
        her single cumulative note . . .

        grief following its image,
        grief's true color vanishing:
        snow on the sleeping volcano.

So it appears on our travels we've seen nothing new,
though I notice how sounds gather daily to undermine the visible:
        blue trees, amber beads, red bird's flight.

All of beauty's evasions,
then the mind's black echo:

Dear Ellipsis,
Dear Night.

ABOUT THE AUTHOR

CAROL MUSKE is the recipient of numerous awards for her poetry, including Guggenheim, NEA, and Ingram-Merrill fellowships. She teaches in the English Department at the University of Southern California and reviews regularly for *The New York Times Book Review*. She lives in Los Angeles with her husband, actor David Dukes, and her daughter, Annie Cameron.